D1585396

Forever Fingerprints

An Amazing Discovery for Adopted Children

SHERRIE ELDRIDGE

Illustrated by Rob Williams

Jessica Kingsley *Publishers*
London and Philadelphia

Dedicated with tons of love to our six unbelievable grandchildren,
Austin, Blake, Cole, Olivia, Eliana, and Megan.
S.E.

To Keira and Isaias...two grand kids.
R.W.

First published in 2007 by EMK Press

This edition published in 2015
by Jessica Kingsley Publishers
73 Collier Street
London N1 9BE, UK
and
400 Market Street, Suite 400
Philadelphia, PA 19106, USA

www.jkp.com

Library of Congress Cataloging in Publication Data
A CIP catalog record for this book is available from the Library of Congress

British Library Cataloguing in Publication Data
Eldridge, Sherrie.
  Forever fingerprints : an amazing discovery for adopted children / Sherrie Eldridge ; illustrations by Rob Williams.
      pages cm
  Originally published by EMK Press in Warren, NJ, 2007.
  Summary: Lucie's aunt and uncle are having a baby which makes Lucie wonder about her birth mother and what it was like before she was born.
  ISBN 978-1-84905-778-3 (alk. paper)
  [1. Adoption--Fiction. 2. Parent and child--Fiction. 3. Birthmothers--Fiction.] I. Williams, Rob, 1951- illustrator. II. Title.
  PZ7.1.E43Fo 2014
  [Fic]--dc23
                            2014021853

ISBN 978 1 84905 778 3
eISBN 978 1 78450 021 4

Printed and bound in China

Dear Parents,

Wouldn't it be great to have someone who could teach you what to say when your child asks deep questions about adoption at a busy traffic intersection? Someone who could help you understand what your child may be thinking about when daydreaming? Someone who could teach you how to create a safe environment for your child to talk freely about adoption?

Seven-year-old Lucie, the main character of this book, along with her adoptive parents, will do that for you! When you see their healthy family dynamics, the nervous discomfort about talking adoption with your child, the fear that your child loves the birth parents more than you, and the fear that you'll say the wrong thing, will all disappear.

You will learn new ways to:

- talk adoption with your child without feeling threatened or nervous
- use everyday circumstances as springboards into meaningful adoption discussions
- handle painful or missing birth history
- be confident about your irreplaceable role in your child's life
- show unconditional love to your child
- enter your child's world and understand his or her perspective about adoption.

As you read Lucie's delightful adoption story, I promise that "talking adoption" with your child will take on a new dimension. You will be looking for those springboards for conversation and feel confident that you are communicating unconditional love to your child. Lucie and her adoption-savvy parents will show you how to talk adoption in a winsome way that will be welcomed by your child.

With warm regards,

Sherrie Eldridge

When Lucie woke up, she remembered that Uncle John and Aunt Grace were coming with a great big surprise. She wiggled her toes, jumped out of bed, and danced into her clothes. Her mom fixed sunshine yellow scrambled eggs, juice, and toast with honey.

But Lucie wasn't hungry because there were butterflies in her tummy.

They will calm down, her mom told her, **if you feed them your breakfast.**

The butterflies ate the scrambled eggs and they drank the juice. They ate everything except the toast with the yummy honey. But the honey was Lucie's favorite part so she scooped it off with her fingers and licked each one—round and round and up and down.

Lucie wanted to look fairy-princess special for her aunt and uncle.

Her lavender dress, high heels, and sparkly crown would be perfect!
Swirling and twirling to music, she dreamed about the **BIG** surprise.

BEEP-beep-beep-beep!

Lucie raced lickety-split to meet them, with arms
stretched high to Aunt Grace for hugs.

BOING BOING!

What was that? She tried again...

BOING-I-TY... BOING... BOING!

WHOA!

It was Aunt Grace's tummy.
It was so **FAT!**
What had she been eating? *Watermelons?*
Uncle John swooped Lucie up in his arms
and whispered the surprise in her ear.
A **REAL** baby was growing inside Aunt Grace's tummy.

YAHOO!

Lucie jumped down, kicked off her high heels,
and turned cartwheels around the yard.

Later, Aunt Grace asked if Lucie wanted to feel the baby.

Lucie's eyes almost popped out of her head when
Aunt Grace pulled up her red blouse.

WOW! Her tummy looked like a beach ball!

Hand-in-hand, they pushed on her tummy.
Lucie felt little taps on her fingertips.

OH MY GOODNESS!

It was the baby tapping on Aunt
Grace's tummy *from the inside!*

All day long Lucie wondered what the baby was doing.
Was he eating?
Was he sleeping?
Was he pooping?

If he was pooping, **where did the poop go?**

Did it turn into pizza?

That night, she moved her
fingertips on her dad's arm,
like an itsy-bitsy spider
going up a water spout. She
wanted to show him how it
felt when the baby kicked.

The next day Lucie and her friend,
Cole, made fingerprint pictures. Lucie
added a head, arms, legs, and feet.

TAAA-DAAA!

It was Aunt Grace's baby!

As they pushed their fingers into the stamp pad and then
onto the paper, they noticed that each of their fingers
made a different print. Some had loops and
some seemed to swirl round and round.

Then Cole noticed that the prints made by Lucie
were different from his.

That night, before bedtime, Lucie dove into bed
and yanked the covers over her head.

Lucie had new questions about her adoption after being with
Aunt Grace and the baby. She knew that everyone has a
birth mother and birth father. She knew she grew in her birth
mother's tummy, and that some kids live with their parents
after they're born and some don't. Lucie had dreamed that her
parents were a king and a queen who lived in a beautiful castle.

But if her birth parents lived in a castle, why didn't they keep her?

Was she too big, too small...did she cry too much, or what?
How could they not love her enough to keep her?
She must have been really **BAD**. Lucie hit her pillow—

Boom! Boom! Boom!

Lucie was sad and screamed that she wanted to grow
in her mom's tummy. She wanted to know whose
fingers had felt her tapping before she was born.

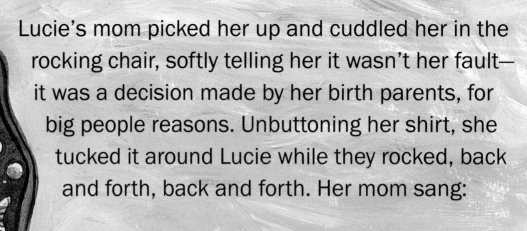

Lucie's mom picked her up and cuddled her in the rocking chair, softly telling her it wasn't her fault—it was a decision made by her birth parents, for big people reasons. Unbuttoning her shirt, she tucked it around Lucie while they rocked, back and forth, back and forth. Her mom sang:

You were and are a good baby,
With perfect fingers and toes,
A head full of soft fuzzy hair,
And an adorable, kissable nose.

Then she wrapped Lucie's hands in hers and blew warm kisses on them.

Lucie asked her dad to tell her again how she got in her birth mother's tummy. He said that there is a special way a man and a woman come together to make babies. Every baby grows in a little pouch called a womb—a place in a mother's body made just for a baby. It stretches as the baby grows, so the little one will always have enough room and always be safe. There is even a warm sack of water around the baby to keep it snug until it is time to be born.

Lucie giggled.
She wondered if the water had fish in it.

Lucie loved thinking about being in her birth mother's womb. *It was her first home.*

The sound of her birth mother's heartbeat made Lucie feel comfy-cozy. All the super-duper things about her birth mother and father were mixed together to make Lucie.

Maybe her love for horses came from her birth father and her pretty-as-a-picture smile from her birth mother?

Lucie asked if she could meet her birth parents. She wanted to know what they were like. Her mom and dad didn't know what they were like or how to find them.

Tears filled Lucie's eyes.
Her mom and dad felt sad, too.

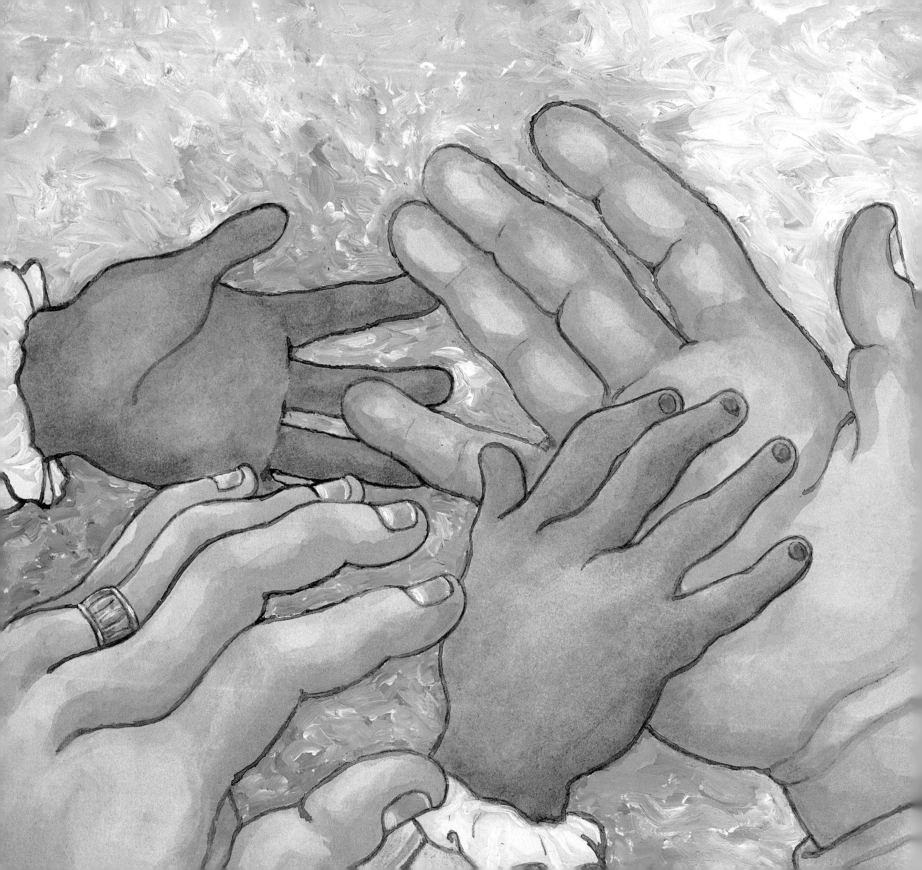

Then her dad grabbed her fingers and told her that they had something special for her—something that they had been waiting for just the right time to tell her...
something about her fingertips.

Lucie's eyes got **BIG!**

Her fingertips had been so busy.

They felt the new baby kick,
and tickled her dad,
and made a fingerprint drawing.

WAIT!

There was **SOMETHING MORE** Lucie had to learn!

No one in the **whole world** has fingerprints exactly like hers. Other parts of her body will change, but not her fingertips. They would be forever the same. Lucie turned her hands upside down and she saw the loops and squiggles of her fingerprints again.

Now her fingertips looked like ten **GOOOOORGEEEOUS** flowers. Lucie grinned from ear-to-ear.

STOP! *Lucie needs to hear the rest of the story!*

The best part about Lucie's fingertips is that they were created while she was so snug inside her birth mother's womb. She was *SO* close to her then and can be close to her *NOW* and *FOREVER.*

HOW? Lucie squealed.

All Lucie needed to do was look at her fingertips and remember her birth mother, just like when she was in her birth mother's womb.

Her fingers would never look the same to her again.

Lucie squeezed her fingertips close together, pushed them to her lips, and planted teeny, tiny kisses on each one. With every kiss, she felt roastier and toastier inside.

Then her parents planted kisses all over her fingertips.

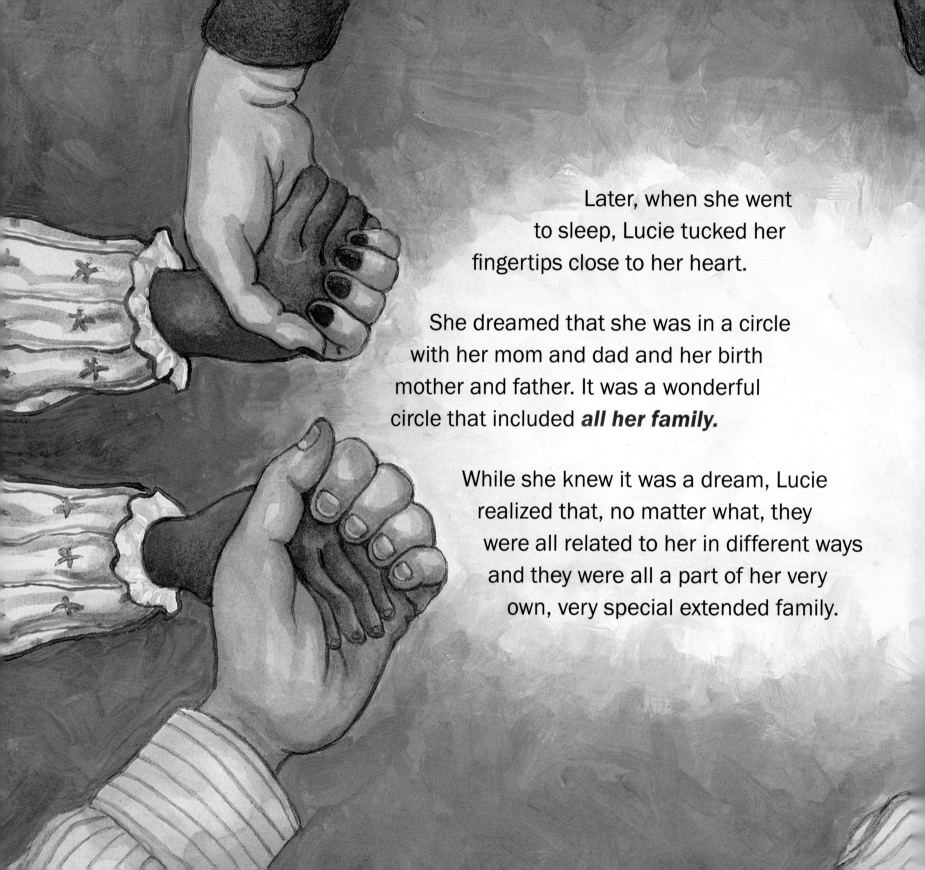

Later, when she went
to sleep, Lucie tucked her
fingertips close to her heart.

She dreamed that she was in a circle
with her mom and dad and her birth
mother and father. It was a wonderful
circle that included **all her family.**

While she knew it was a dream, Lucie
realized that, no matter what, they
were all related to her in different ways
and they were all a part of her very
own, very special extended family.

Using Forever Fingerprints: Parent Tools and Activities

As you read *Forever Fingerprints*, you will see there is more to the sweet story of connection that Sherrie Eldridge created than meets the eye. It's about how babies grow in their moms' tummies, and how adopted children have a forever connection to their birth parents through their fingertips. It's a wonderful tool to open the door for more loving conversations and truthful discussions about how you and your child came to be a family.

As any child grows, they wonder about their beginnings. As our adopted children grow, the answers to basic questions such as, "Did I grow in your tummy, Mommy?" lead us to start discussions about their adoption stories, and how the baby got in there. For all children this is a normal part of figuring out their place in the family—often a pregnant relative or friend will be the springboard for these discussions, like with Lucie and her Aunt Grace. For many of us parents, this is the dreaded discussion.

If we introduce them to birth parents, will they love and want them more? The reality is that kids know who all the parts of their families are and are able to make sense of different relationships. They know who takes care of them and loves them every day.

And they depend on us, as their parents, to help them to make sense of something that can be pretty hard to understand when you are 5 or 6 or 7—the concept of adoption and the bittersweetness that surrounds it. To get the family they have, another family had to give them up. That can be tough stuff for our children and we need to know how to catch them, like Lucie's parents, in a supportive and loving way that is open to any discussion our children need to have with us. We wholeheartedly claim our children, but in claiming all the parts of them, including their extended families—their birth families—our circle of love and understanding is expanded, not diminished.

We suggest that you read this book first, to help prepare you for questions that might arise during the reading or after.

So what questions might arise as children read this book with you?

Some of the questions that you may find will be "what-ifs"—questions about what it would be like if your child had stayed with his or her birth family. They also may be about your child's yearning to meet birth parents and learn more about what they are like. Some questions may be about your child's grief and anger at loss—the loss of their birth family and the chance to be parented by the people who gave birth to them. Other questions might be about their place in the family, who their relatives are and how it all fits. For some children, this book will bring to life the very real understanding that they were born. Many have heard their adoption story, but not their birth story.

And what questions might arise for you as you read this book?

As parents, we need to come to terms with the parts of the story of how our children came to be with us that are hard to hear or that trigger our own feelings.

Pregnancy questions can be hard for those who have experienced infertility. Suggesting a connection between yourself and your child's birth parents might be hard. You might be concerned by the idea of connection, either real or emotional. There may be hard truths in the past of your child and the reality of the story may be difficult to deal with. Or your child may have birth siblings who are currently being parented by his or her birth parents. There could be many difficult truths that stop us as parents from talking about our children's past and their birth history. It is our job to make sense of our own issues so that we can move beyond them and help our children. Tools like this book can help both parent and child.

Reading the book

Some children will stop you as you read to ask questions; others will ponder and raise their questions later. Still others might feel out of sorts and cover that up with silliness, like Lucie does. Every child is different. Older children may listen keenly as the book is read to a younger sibling, taking their own understanding of the information presented. Other children will read the story over and over looking for things hidden in the pictures and in the words. Being able to hold our children close and answer any questions they have with honesty and love is the most important gift we can give them. Each time you read this story, your child will come away with a little more.

Activities for later

You may want to use fingerprint stamping as a tool for further discussion. The fingerprint tool is powerful and art is a marvellous way to describe feelings and thoughts too complicated for words to young children. You may want to talk with your children about feelings and loss—use daily life for this, such as the loss of a pet, or disagreements with school friends or siblings. Another useful way to talk to your child about connections is to use lifebooks, pictures, and photos that relate to their pre-adoption history.

Forever Fingerprints offers more, much more, for you and your adopted child. It can be read on many levels—as a simple story or as a springboard narrative for you and your child to ponder further on birth parents. It can start you on the path of developing narratives about your child's connection to his or her birth family and to you. This book allows us to explore the fears both we and our children have about being an adoptive family. It allows us to celebrate the joy that being connected brings.

We parents share that gift with our children by helping them understand that they are safe with us, and safe in the understanding that we can help them to navigate the big feelings that adoption can bring.

Carrie Kitze and Sheena Macrae
Publishers of the original edition

A little something about fingerprints...

The outer layer of skin on our fingers has a series of ridges on it forming special patterns we call fingerprints. Everybody has a special-to-them set of fingerprints and patterns can run in families. Fingerprint ridges form on a baby's fingers while in the womb, around the third and fourth months of development. Identical twins start out with the same general patterns on their fingertips, but differences in the patterns are created according to how fast they grow inside their mom, their position in the womb, and how much they move around.

Once fully developed, the pattern of ridges never change, even as each finger grows. Think about drawing a picture on a balloon and then blowing it up. The picture just grows larger but doesn't change. That's what happens to your fingerprints as you grow.

There are three main patterns that are found on fingertips: the arch, the loop, and the whorl. Which kinds do you have? The loop is the most common. In some families, people have the same kinds of patterns on the same fingers, which means that fingerprints are hereditary. Hereditary means that some physical characteristic is passed from biological parent to child. If you have a swirl on one of your fingertips, either your birth mom or birth dad might have that too. The size of your fingertips and the shape of them has a lot to do with what basic pattern appears on your finger.

The best way to see what your fingerprints look like is to use a stamp pad. Be careful not to smudge them! Have an adult help you to roll a finger on a stamp pad. Then repeat the process on clean white paper. Make sure you clean your fingers before you touch other things. Your parents have experience with fingerprinting because they had to have their fingerprints taken as part of the paperwork to adopt you!

You can make fun figures with fingerprints. There are some ideas scattered in this book. What can you think of to make?

whorl

loop

arch

Free fingerprint craft sheets and Adoption Ceremony are available to download from my site: www.SherrieEldridge.com.